Morgan's Baby Sister

A Read-Aloud Book for Families Who Have Experienced the Death of a Newborn

Patricia Polin Johnson • Donna Reilly Williams

Illustrated by
Suzanne Schaffhausen

Resource Publications, Inc.
San Jose, California

Editorial director: Kenneth Guentert
Managing editor: Elizabeth J. Asborno
Cover design: Suzanne Schaffhausen, Huey Lee
Cover production: Huey Lee
Patricia Polin Johnson's photo by: Mark Comon

Library of Congress Cataloging in Publication Data
Johnson, Patricia Polin, 1956-
Morgan's baby sister : a read-aloud book for families who have experienced the death of a newborn / Patricia Polin Johnson, Donna Reilly Williams ; illustrated by Suzanne Schaffhausen.
p. cm. — (Helping children who hurt)
Summary: Morgan tries to sort out and understand her feelings when her family's excited preparations for a new baby end with unexpected tragedy.
[1. Death—Fiction. 2. Pregnancy—Fiction. 3. Babies—Fiction.] I. Williams, Donna Reilly, 1945- . II. Schaffhausen, Suzanne, ill. III. Title. IV. Series.
PZ7.J63535Mo 1993
[E]—dc20 93-11996

97 96 95 94 93 | 5 4 3 2 1

To A.J., and Baby J,
for the joy you've brought into my life.
— P.P.J.

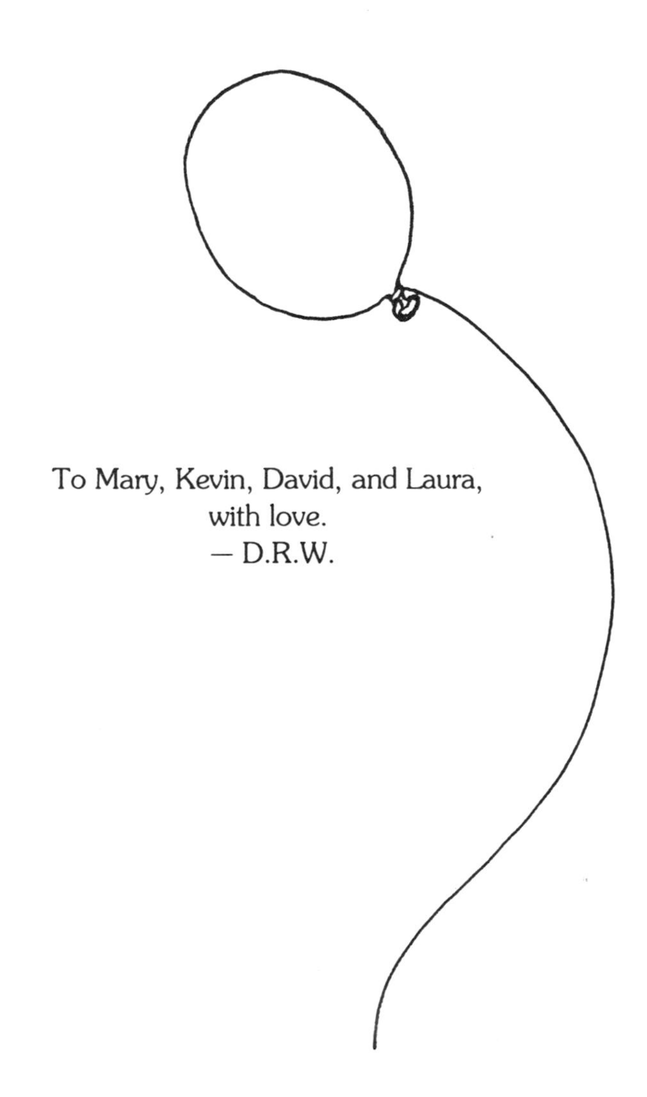

To Mary, Kevin, David, and Laura,
with love.
— D.R.W.

Contents

Morgan's Baby Sister

I.

Morgan placed her doll, Suzanne, on the chair next to her at the dinner table. She felt happy because Mommy had cooked baked chicken with mashed potatoes, Morgan's favorite dinner.

"Morgan," said Mommy. "Have you ever wanted a real baby?"

Morgan thought for a moment. Suzanne was very nice, but she couldn't talk or drink from a bottle like a real baby.

"Could I play with it?" she asked.

Daddy chuckled. "Well, after she's grown a little," he said.

"I'd like that," Morgan answered.

Mommy smiled at Morgan. "I'm so glad," she said. "Because you *are* going to have a baby sister."

"I am?"

Morgan thought some more. "Will she come from a hospital, like Steven's brother did?" she asked.

"Oh, Morgan," Mommy laughed. "When it comes time for her to be born, the doctors and nurses at the hospital will help. But our baby is already here."

"Where?" asked Morgan. She wondered if Daddy and Mommy were teasing her.

“Babies start out very tiny, smaller than your pinky finger,” Mommy explained. “They’re too little to live in the world like you and I do. So at first, they grow inside their mothers until they’re ready to be born.”

Morgan thought about that. It was strange to think about a baby inside of a mother.

“Did I grow inside of you, Mommy?” she asked.

“Yes, Morgan, you did,” answered Mommy.

“And is our new baby inside of you now?” Morgan’s voice was very small because this was such a big question.

Mommy got up and came to kneel beside Morgan’s chair. She placed Morgan’s hand on her tummy.

Suddenly, Morgan felt something. It was not really a bump. But something was moving inside Mommy.

Morgan’s eyes popped open very wide, and she whispered, “Is that our baby?”

“Yes, Sweetie. Can you feel her kicking?” Morgan nodded her head, and she felt the tiny bump again.

“Maybe she’s trying to say ‘hello’ to her big sister,” said Daddy.

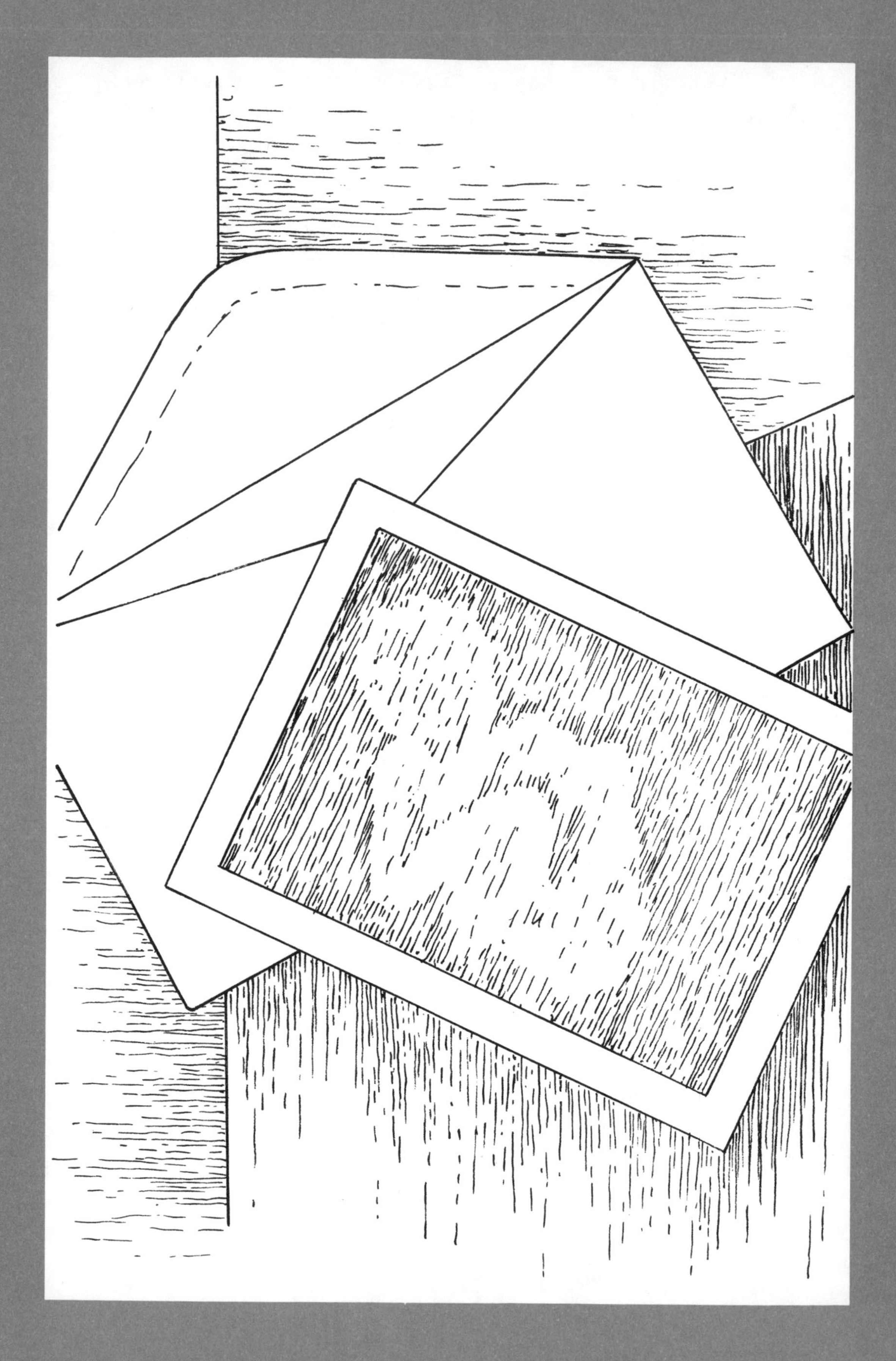

"When can we really see her?" Morgan asked.

Daddy walked over to the sideboard and picked up an envelope. "We can't see her for quite a while yet, Honey. But we have a picture of her for you."

Out of the envelope, he pulled a funny picture of black and gray lines and shadows. Morgan looked at the picture. It sure didn't look like any baby she had ever seen.

"Is this her?" she asked.

"This is a photograph the doctor took with a special camera," Daddy explained. "It shows you how our baby is lying inside Mommy. Here's her head, and this looks like a foot. The picture isn't too clear because the camera had to see through Mommy's skin."

"Is this her leg?" Morgan asked, pointing to the photograph.

"It must be," answered Mommy.

Morgan held the picture and thought. "We have sharing day tomorrow," she said. "Could I take this picture and show it to my class?"

Daddy smiled and looked at Mommy. "Of course you may, Honey," he said.

That night, Morgan dreamed about her new baby sister dancing inside Mommy.

The next day, she explained the picture to her first-grade class.

"What's the baby's name?" Mary Beth MacDonald asked.

"I don't know," Morgan said.

"Well, everyone has a name," Mary Beth insisted.

"I'm sure they'll select a very nice name, Mary Beth," said Mr. Wojinski. "What other things will they do to prepare for Morgan's new sister?"

"They need plenty of diapers," said Marta. She had a baby brother.

"My mom and dad had to fix up a bedroom when they got me," said Morgan's best friend, Krissy.

"When we got my little brother, we had to take the Christmas decorations out of the closet in his room," said Yolanda.

"They have to have a party for Morgan's mom," Tony added.

"That's right," said Walter. "With cake and ice cream and presents."

"They have to give the baby a name," said Mary Beth MacDonald.

That night, Morgan told Mommy and Daddy about the things her class said.

"What *are* we going to name her?" she asked.

"Why don't we choose a name together?" Mommy said.

"How about 'Suzanne', like my doll?" Morgan asked.

"Maybe we should pick a different name, so your Suzanne won't be confused," suggested Daddy. "How about 'Ezmiralda', like my great-aunt?"

"Ugh!" said Morgan. "Ez-mi-ral-da!"

"That's such a big name for a little baby!" laughed Mommy.

Morgan was thinking. "Our class just read a story," she said, "about a girl who was brave and smart and beautiful and friendly. Her name was Marissa."

"Marissa," repeated Mommy. "That's a beautiful name."

"I like it too," agreed Daddy.

"Then Marissa Montgomery it is!" exclaimed Mommy.

Saturday arrived a few days later, and Daddy asked Morgan to help him in the attic.

"I've got something I want you to see," he said. He lifted a big piece of canvas.

"Oh," whispered Morgan. "Whose is it?"

Daddy came over to Morgan and took her in his arms.

"This is *your* crib, Honey. Mommy and I were wondering if Marissa could use it."

Morgan thought about herself sleeping in that crib when she was very small. She couldn't remember how it had felt.

Then she thought of their new baby, Marissa.

"Okay, Daddy," she said slowly. "Do you think we should paint it?"

"That's a great idea!" Daddy said, giving Morgan a kiss. "You're a wonderful big sister!"

The next few weeks brought many changes to the Montgomery household.

They decided to change the extra bedroom into Marissa's nursery.

Daddy painted Morgan's old baby furniture, and Morgan and Krissy tied pink ribbons all over the crib.

Marissa was changing, too. Daddy told Morgan that, inside Mommy, Marissa had fingernails and little tufts of hair. As Marissa grew, Mommy's tummy grew, too.

Every day, Morgan said, "Good morning, Marissa," to Mommy's tummy.

Every evening after dinner, Morgan, Daddy, and Mommy with Marissa, walked. They talked about the things they would do when Marissa was born.

"You can help her learn to walk," Mommy told Morgan.

"And talk," added Daddy.

"I can hold her," Morgan said. "And I can help her say her prayers every night."

"And you can teach her how to tie bows, use scissors, and blow soap bubbles," Mommy said.

"She has so much to learn!" Morgan exclaimed.

The next day, Mommy saw Morgan showing Suzanne how to tie her shoes.

"I'm practicing, so I can teach Marissa," Morgan told Mommy.

"You're a wonderful big sister!" Mommy said.

II.

One dark night, Daddy gently shook Morgan awake. "Wake up, honey," Daddy said.

"I'm sleepy," Morgan moaned.

"Morgan, I need you to wake up. Something is wrong. Marissa is getting ready to be born right now, but it's too soon. I'm taking Mommy to the hospital," said Daddy. Morgan knew this was important because Daddy was using his special-occasion voice.

Morgan picked up Suzanne and stumbled out of bed. She could hear Mommy in the living room, talking to Krissy's mom.

"Thanks so much, Valerie," Mommy was saying. "Dr. Adams told me to go in right away."

"Try not to worry," Mrs. Travis said. "I'll take care of Morgan. You just take care of yourself and the baby."

Mrs. Travis took Morgan to her house and helped her climb into bed beside Krissy. Morgan fell right to sleep.

"Mommy's never stayed away overnight before," Morgan told Krissy the next morning.

"Maybe she's coming home with your dad," Krissy said.

They heard a car door slam and ran to look.

"It's only Daddy," Morgan said as they watched him walk slowly to the front door.

Daddy didn't say much at Krissy's house. He thanked Krissy's mom for keeping Morgan, and he held Morgan's hand as they walked to the car.

Morgan was scared. She had never seen her daddy like this. And where was Mommy? And Marissa?

When they got home, Daddy sat in the big blue chair and took Morgan on his lap. She leaned her head against his chest and she could feel his heart beating.

Finally, Daddy spoke, very softly and slowly.

"Morgan, I have something to tell you. It's about Marissa."

"Where is she?" Morgan asked. "Was she born in the night?"

"Yes, Honey," continued Daddy. "Marissa was born, and she had blonde hair, like you, and big blue eyes.

"But then, in the night, she got very sick, so sick that the doctors couldn't help her or make her better."

Marissa didn't know what to think. "But what did they do?" she asked.

"Well, they tried a lot of things. You see, Honey, Marissa wasn't really ready to be born, and she couldn't breathe. The doctors tried helping her with a special breathing machine. But her little body just couldn't go on living.

"Morgan, Marissa is in heaven now, with God. Only God could make her better. But God couldn't do it here. So she had to go to heaven. She can breathe in heaven, but she couldn't breathe here." Daddy's voice was choked. He sounded like he could hardly talk.

"But I never got to hold her!" Morgan cried. "And she never used the crib or all the clothes we got for her."

"Someday, Morgan," said Daddy, "we'll all go to heaven, and then we'll see Marissa. But that won't be for a long time. Most people don't go to heaven until they're very old."

Morgan thought a long time, leaning against Daddy and listening to his heart. Then she sat up.

"Where's Mommy?" she asked.

"Mommy's at the hospital," Daddy said. "She's coming home tomorrow. Marissa's illness made her very tired, and the doctor wants her to rest. She'll be fine in a few days, but we all feel very sad and lonely for Marissa."

"Marissa!" Morgan cried.

Daddy held Morgan as she cried and cried. Daddy cried, too.

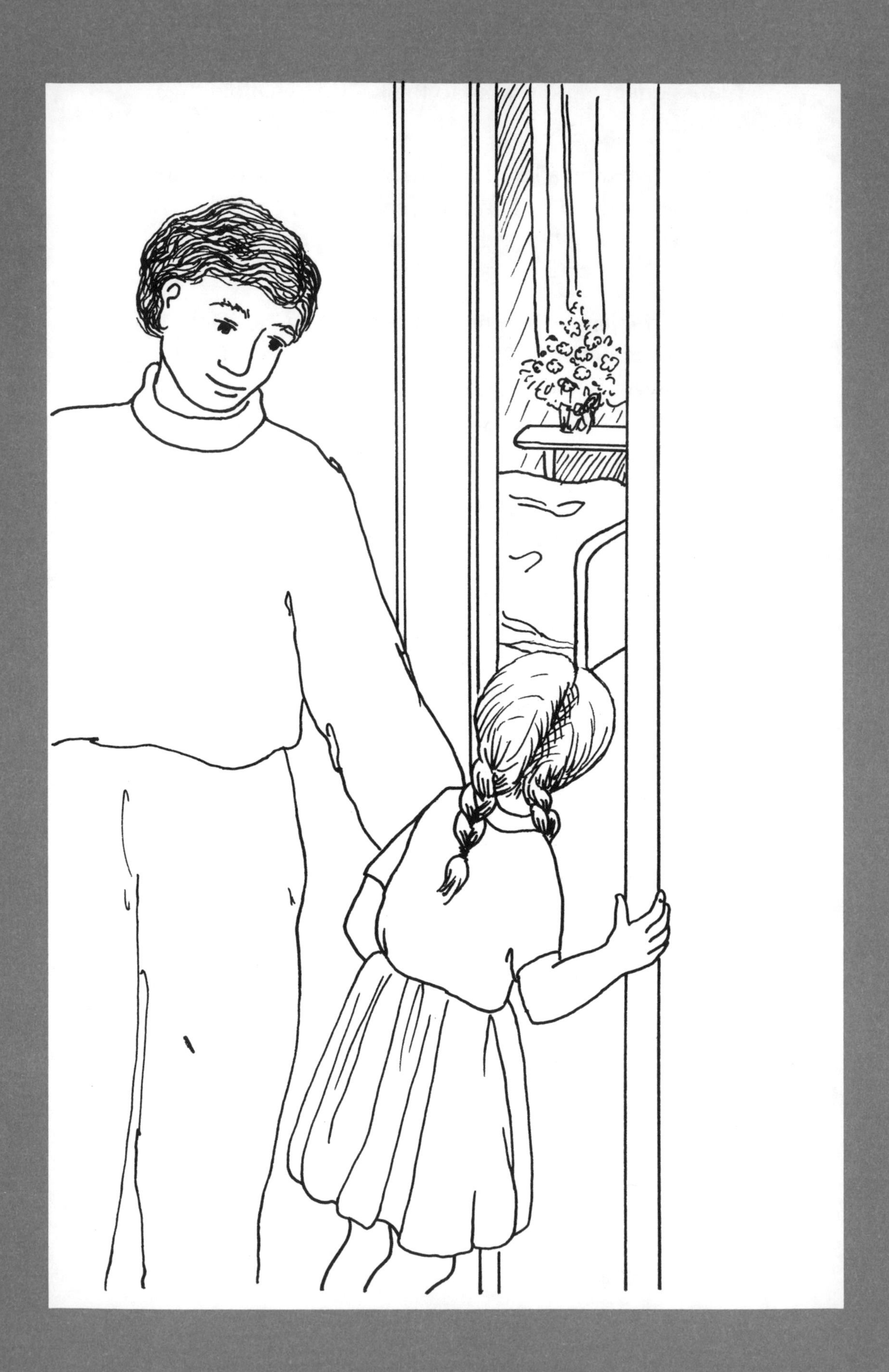

Later that day, Mrs. Travis stopped by to see Morgan and Daddy.

"How's Ann feeling?" she asked.

Morgan sat quietly and hugged Suzanne.

"She's feeling better," Daddy said. "I'll bring her home tomorrow."

"Shall I watch Morgan for you?" asked Mrs. Travis.

"I want to get Mommy, too," said Morgan quickly. "I want to be with you, Daddy."

"I think Mommy would want you to play with Krissy tomorrow, instead of waiting for her to check out of the hospital," said Daddy. "But why don't we go to visit her right now?"

At the hospital, Morgan couldn't resist peeking into each room they passed. Finally, Daddy stopped at room 368 and pushed open the door.

"Hello, Mommy," Morgan whispered.

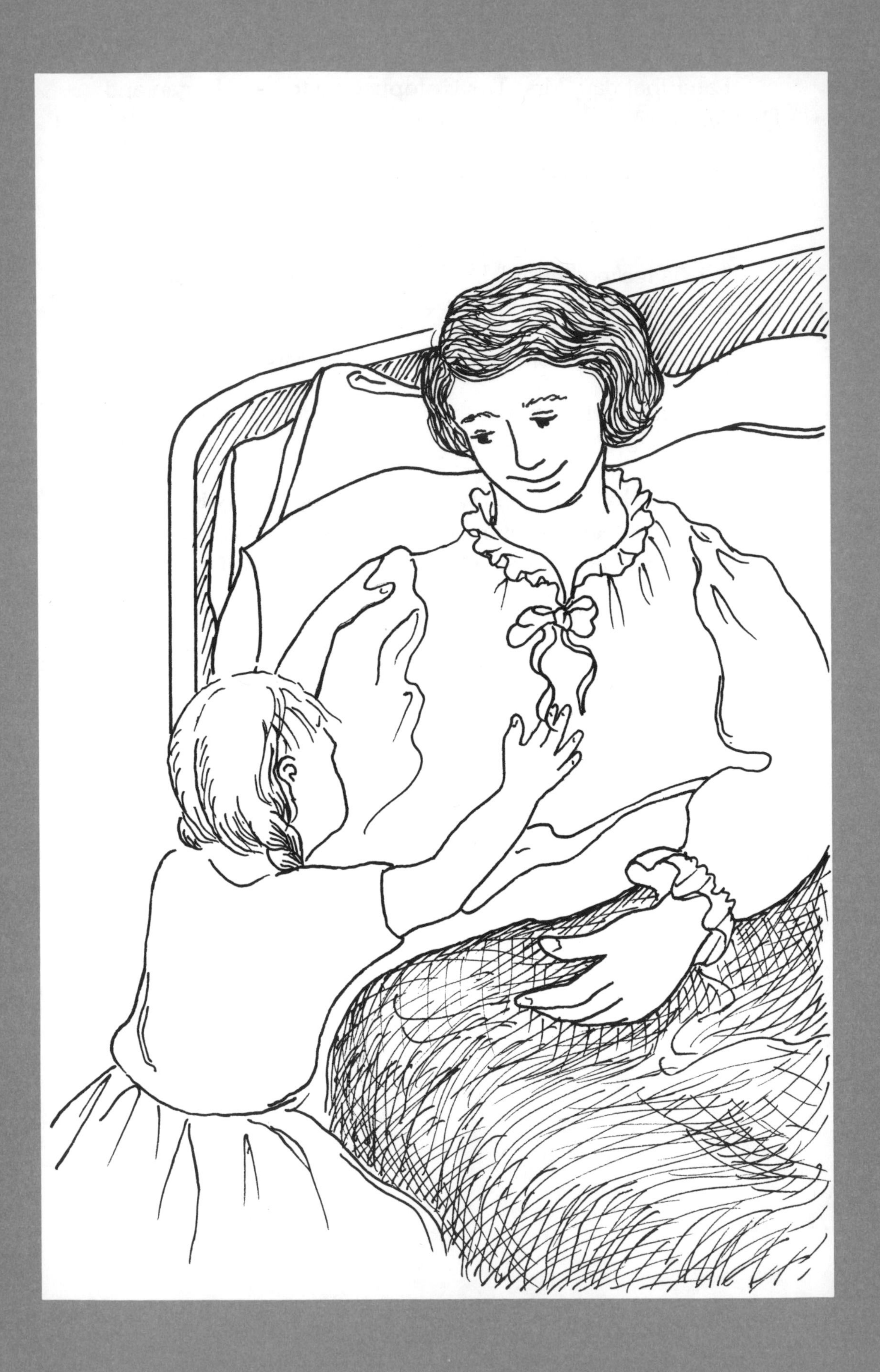

Mommy was in a big bed. She looked pretty, propped against the pillows. She put out her arms, and Morgan climbed up onto the bed.

"How are you, Honey?" asked Mommy. "I missed you!"

"Are you okay, Mommy?" asked Morgan. "When are you coming home?"

"I'm fine, Honey. I just need to rest," Mommy said.

Daddy showed Morgan around Mommy's room. There was a closet, and lots of strange shiny things were on the wall. And a bathroom was right next door.

In a few minutes, Daddy said, "Maybe we'd better go now, Morgan. You and Mommy both need to get to sleep early tonight."

The next morning, Daddy took Morgan to Krissy's house. He was going to the hospital.

"Hug Mommy for me," Morgan said.

"I'll do better than that," answered Daddy. "I'll bring her home so you can hug her yourself."

"Come on, Morgan," said Krissy. "Let's go play catch."

"I don't feel like playing right now," Morgan said.

"I have some gingerbread dough," said Mrs. Travis. "Why don't you both help me make some cookies?"

Krissy ran into the kitchen and began shaping her dough into a baseball player. Morgan trailed behind her.

"I was thinking, Morgan," said Krissy. "At least now you don't have to share Suzanne with a little sister."

"I wouldn't have minded sharing her with Marissa," said Morgan.

"Maybe," said Krissy. "Still, I'm glad I don't have a baby sister who always needs clean diapers."

Mrs. Travis spoke. "Krissy, you never knew this, but when you were about a year old, your daddy and I found out you were going to have a baby sister."

Morgan and Krissy both looked at Krissy's mom.

"What happened to her?" asked Morgan.

"She got very sick, too, just like your baby, Morgan, and she went to be with God." Morgan could see that there were shiny tears in Mrs. Travis' eyes.

"You mean I have a little sister in heaven, just like Morgan?" asked Krissy.

"That's right," said her mom.

Morgan looked at her friend. She could tell Krissy was thinking.

"I would have taught her how to play baseball, and I would have pushed her on the swings," said Krissy. "I even would have played house with her, if she wanted."

Mrs. Travis went to Krissy and took her hand. She looked straight into her eyes, and she kissed Krissy's hand, gingerbread dough and all.

"You would have been a wonderful big sister," she said. "But our baby was just too sick to live."

"Just like Marissa," said Morgan.

"Just like Marissa," said Mrs. Travis. She reached over and held Morgan's hand, too.

"But I never got to see my sister," said Krissy.

"You will, someday," Morgan said quietly. "We both will someday, a long time from now. Maybe, right now, Marissa and your baby sister are playing together in heaven, just like we are here."

Just then, they heard a car door, and Morgan ran to meet Mommy and Daddy.

Mommy gently took Morgan's hand, and they both went home with Daddy. When they walked into their house, Mommy dropped to her knees and wrapped her arms around Morgan.

"My little Morgan," Mommy said. "I love you very, very much." Mommy held Morgan a long time.

Morgan began to cry.

"Mommy," she said, "I want Marissa to come home!"

"I know, Sweetie," said Mommy. "I want that, too. But it can't happen. Marissa couldn't live here, because her body couldn't breathe. She's so much better with God taking care of her in heaven."

"Did you say goodbye to her?" Morgan asked.

"No." Mommy looked at Morgan. "I... I didn't think of it." Her voice was soft and sad.

"I wish I could have said goodbye to her," Morgan said.

That night, Morgan heard Mommy and Daddy crying in their bedroom. Morgan cried herself to sleep.

III.

The next day, Daddy cooked dinner. Mommy had rested on the sofa all day. When they were sitting at the table, Mommy asked a question.

"What would you think if we had a memorial service for Marissa? We could celebrate the joy she brought to our family and," she smiled at Morgan, "we could also say goodbye to her."

"I've heard of people doing that," Daddy said. "We could invite our close friends, and our folks."

"What's a 'morial service?" asked Morgan.

"That's when all the people who loved a person get together," answered Daddy. "They help each other with their sadness, and they pray for each other and for the person who has died."

"Could I invite Krissy?" Morgan asked.

"Of course, and her family too," Mommy answered.

Morgan thought for a moment.

"Mommy and Daddy, did you know that Krissy also has a baby sister in heaven?" she asked.

Mommy and Daddy looked surprised.

"No, I never knew that," said Mommy. "They never mentioned it to us."

"Well, she does," said Morgan. She felt very grown-up.

"That's why they seem able to understand what we're going through," said Daddy.

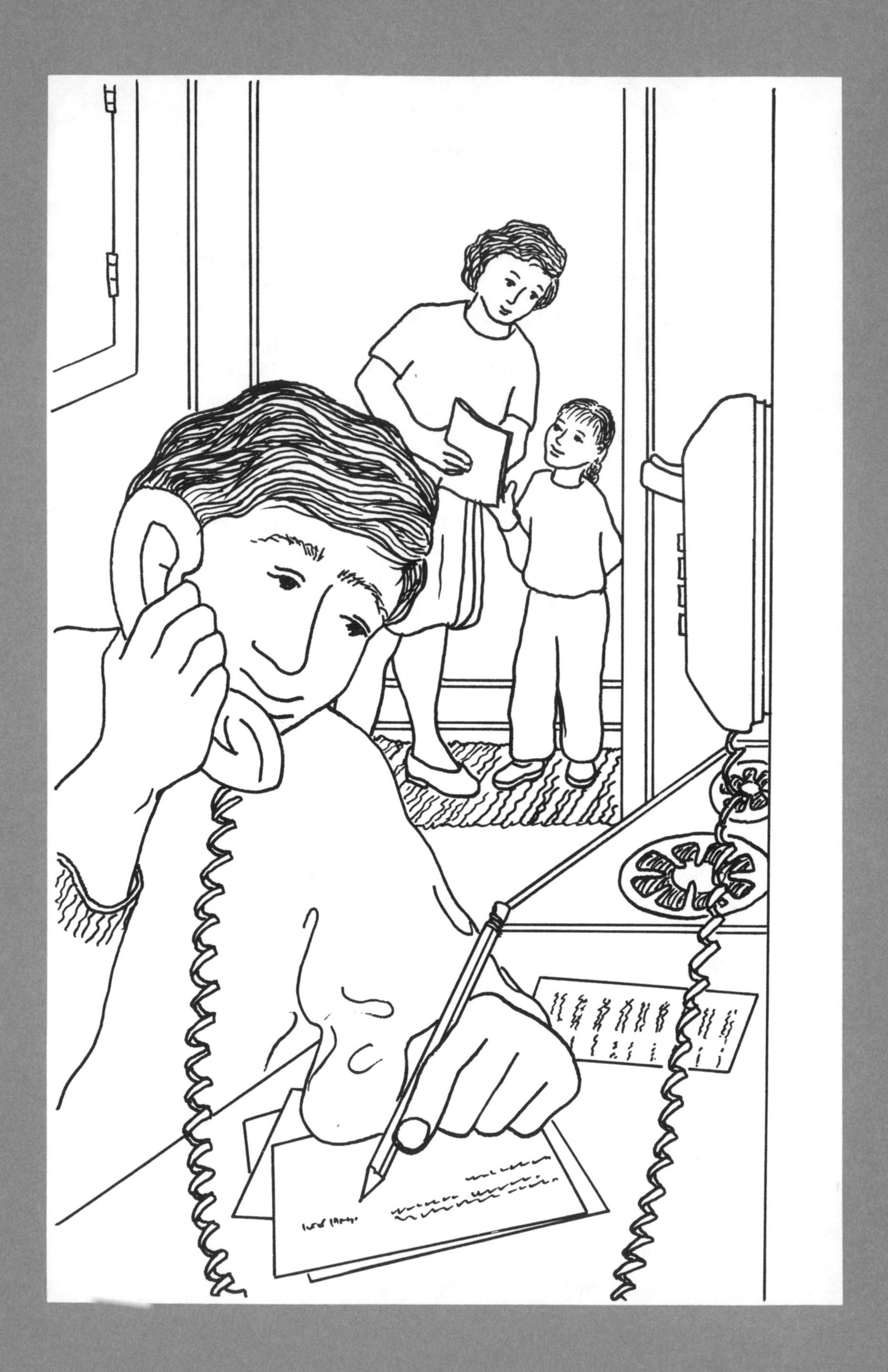

Mommy looked at Morgan and smiled.

"How do you know about this?" she asked.

"Mrs. Travis told me and Krissy when we were making cookies," explained Morgan. "Krissy never knew 'til just then, either. I think Krissy felt sad, like we feel about Marissa. And I think Mrs. Travis was crying a little."

Mommy and Daddy looked sad. Daddy nodded his head and Mommy said, "Poor things, never talking about it, in all the time we've known them."

Morgan had an idea.

"Mommy and Daddy," she said, "could Krissy say hello *and* goodbye to her baby sister at the service we have for Marissa?"

Mommy looked surprised. Daddy was looking down at the table. They didn't speak for a few minutes. Morgan was beginning to wonder if she had said something wrong.

Then Mommy and Daddy looked at each other, and Daddy nodded, just a little bit. Mommy spoke.

"Yes, Honey," she said. "That would be the perfect time for Krissy to say hello and goodbye to her little sister."

That night, they sat together in the living room and planned the memorial service. It would be the next Sunday. They began to invite their friends, and Grandma and Grandpa and Uncle Bert.

On the day of the service, a lot of people came. They brought flowers and food. All the food went into the kitchen. When everyone was there, they all sat in the living room. Morgan sat on Daddy's lap and Krissy was sitting between her parents. Mommy was sitting beside Grandma, holding her hand.

Pastor Bill began to speak.

"Bless our two little babies, Lord, and keep them in your loving care, until someday, when we will all join you in heaven, too."

Mommy read from the Bible, and Daddy read his favorite poem about little girls.

Daddy and Krissy's dad helped the girls light the two pink candles they had picked out at the store.

Everyone said a prayer for Marissa and for Krissy's sister, whom Krissy had named "Joanna." Then they all walked to the backyard, where there was a big bouquet of pink balloons. Earlier in the day, Morgan and Krissy had helped their parents fill the balloons from a big tank of helium.

They untied the bouquet, and everybody in the family got to hold a balloon.

Pastor Bill said, "These balloons are helping us say goodbye to Marissa and Joanna. You may hold onto your balloons for as long as you want, and when you are ready to say goodbye, you can let them go."

Daddy and Morgan were standing together, and they held both of their balloons together.

Morgan looked up at Daddy, and Daddy said, "Are you ready, Morgan?"

Morgan felt very sad inside, but she looked up at the beautiful balloons and she told Daddy, "Now I'm ready."

As Daddy and Morgan released the strings from their hands, their balloons floated up into the sky, riding the wind and growing smaller and smaller. With them were all the other balloons.

"Goodbye, Marissa. Goodbye, Joanna."

"Maybe the balloons will fly all the way to heaven," said Krissy. "Maybe Marissa and Joanna will catch them."

Then everyone went inside and shared a meal. Their friends made sure that Mommy ate. Daddy served himself. Morgan and Krissy picked at their food in the kitchen.

After an hour or two, their friends began to leave.

"Ann, call me if you need anything," Mrs. Mancini told Mommy.

Mr. Stevens shook Daddy's hand. "You've got to be strong now, Mark," he said.

Mrs. Jackson talked to Morgan in the kitchen. "Play quietly now, Sweetie, because your mommy needs her rest."

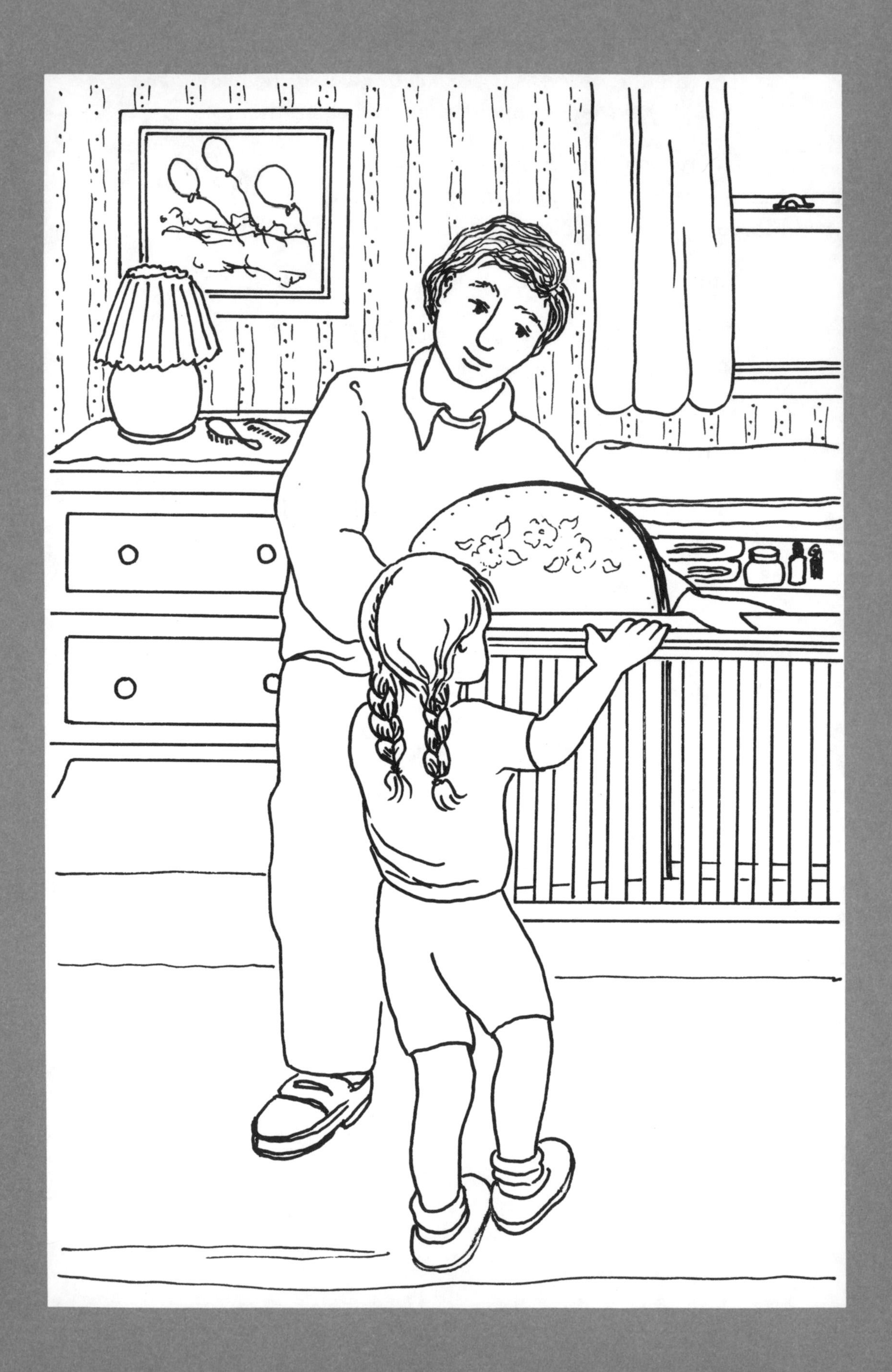

For a few days after the service, their friends brought over food, and others called to offer help. Finally, no one came over. Things were quiet again.

One day, a few weeks later, Daddy called, "Morgan, I need your help in here."

Morgan stepped into Marissa's nursery.

"I think we'd better take this back into the attic," Daddy said.

Morgan bit her lip and nodded. Then she started to untie the pink ribbons that she and Krissy had put on the corners of the crib.

They both worked quietly, folding the crib. Then they took it into the attic and covered it with a big cloth.

Morgan was thinking as she worked. It had been a long time since Marissa had gone to heaven.

"Daddy, why are we all still so sad?" she asked.

Daddy knelt down and pressed Morgan to himself.

“I think it’s because we love Marissa, and we miss having her with us,” he said. His voice had that strange, hurting sound, and Morgan knew he understood how she felt.

“Is it bad to talk about her?” she asked.

“Oh, no, Morgan,” said Daddy. “Marissa is still part of our family. She always will be. Even if someday we have another baby, Marissa will still be your little sister.”

“And she’s waiting for us in heaven, right?” Morgan asked.

“That’s right, Honey,” Daddy said.

“But is it okay to still cry?” asked Morgan.

Mommy had been watching from the doorway. Now, she came over and put her arms around both Morgan and Daddy.

“Yes, Honey,” she said. “It’s fine to cry. In fact, I think it sometimes helps.”

“Will you always love me?” Morgan asked.

“We will love you forever,” they both said, and gave Morgan a big, long hug.

To the Caregiver

The HELPING CHILDREN WHO HURT series is designed to assist adult caregivers with the difficult and often painful task of helping children understand their own feelings about tragedies they experience.

One of the hardest tasks of helping children lies in moving past our own understandings of life and into the space of the child. We who care for children understand that they often do not perceive and interpret life events in the same ways adults do. But often, we do not know *how* their thinking process and feelings are operating. And, children being children, they usually are not able to explain their own experiences. So all the well-meant attention in the world can be wasted because we are not able to communicate.

These little books will help with that communication. They will stimulate discussion and encourage both adult and child to examine and share their own experiences. The hints in this guidebook will give some useful insights to adult caregivers and will help you find direction for your conversations. There are no rules about how to use the books; our suggestions are meant only to serve as beginnings. For some, the presence of the questions will provide courage to begin to address areas which otherwise would have been full of mystique and fear. No more will parents need to say, "I know I need to speak with my child about ______, but I don't know how to begin." No more will teachers need to think, "Johnny must be upset about ______, but how do I reach out to him?" Now, the HELPING CHILDREN WHO HURT books will help you to begin.

The series is designed to respond especially to the needs and development of four- to eight-year-old children. This is an age when children are perceiving and reacting to life in many obvious ways but are usually not able to understand or explain their responses. Adults who care for and about them may ache for their pain but not know how to reach out and support.

Be a Caring Presence

The first thing to remember is that your presence is probably the most important factor. Constancy, fidelity—these are not just old-fashioned words. They are the base upon which any relationship with children must be built. If a child knows that you can be depended upon, that you will be faithful in the relationship, he will then believe that he is important to you. And if the child believes that you really care, then he will begin to trust you, even with the scary experiences which are so hard to understand.

Don't expect that you can just turn up at a tough time and speak some words of wisdom which will help the child's pain and bond the two of you forever. Even the most competent therapist knows that these things take time. The child will need to interact with you—"feel you out"—and decide if you are reliable and trustworthy. One term to describe this reality is "investment." The child will check whether you are really invested in the relationship, or if it is not very important to you.

The other mistake adults often make—once they know they need a "relationship" before the child will allow them to break into the painful areas—is to become a "smotherer." The thought process is something like this, "I want to help this child, so first I'll *prove* that I'm a friend."

Respect the Child's Boundaries

Children, like adults, have boundaries, but often, children are not as good as older people at defining those boundaries to others. They need to be respected. Always use the same respectful voice and stance with a child in pain as you would with an adult. If you want to touch the child, make sure your touch is wanted. If you are not sure, ask, "I'd really like a hug right now. Would that be okay with you?"

Listen!

The ideal, of course, is that you already have a relationship with the child who is hurting. Even then, you may not know how to talk about that specific area of life which is causing the pain. Take the book and sit in a quiet place together. Then tell the child, "I think what has been happening to your family is really awful. If I were you, I think I'd be pretty mixed up. Is that how you feel?" Then really listen. The child may not be as confused as you think, or she may share some of her confusion with you. When you have listened, affirm the questions and also the answers which the child has worked out. Those answers likely "fit" that child's life needs and must be respected.

At this point, tell the child that you have found a book about a family which experienced something like she is experiencing. Say that you'd like to read the book with her and that she can tell you if she thinks it is realistic. This sort of approach values the child's insights and encourages her to really listen to the story.

Don't try to analyze the child's answers or give solutions. Most painful situations can't be "fixed"; they can only be survived. And children, like adults, usually find courage and strength to survive through compassionate support from another person. The most supportive message you can give a child is that whatever he is feeling, he has a friend who will try to understand. If he is angry or frustrated or terribly sad, tell him those feelings are normal, given what he is going through.

Allow the Child to Grieve

Often, adults think that children should always be happy. A grandparent dies, a puppy is killed by a car, Mommy and Dad separate, and adults tell the child that everything will be fine. We justify Granny's death by saying "Old people die, you know." We bring home a new puppy and expect the child to immediately love it. We say, "Don't worry. Mommy and Dad both still love you, so you won't be hurt or affected by this."

In reality, childhood is no more a happy time than is adulthood. In fact, because children have much less control over circumstances and far fewer life experiences upon which they can reflect when crisis comes, these times are often more traumatic for them than for adults. Think back on your own childhood. Were you always happy? We (the authors) have never met a person who was. Children, like adults, are experiencing life, with all its ups and downs. We need to allow them their own feelings and validate their journeys.

So be sure that, whatever the child expresses, you assure her that she is normal. You might want to share with her about something in your life which made you feel as she does today. That will establish her sense of your empathy; it will also help her know that she can get through this time because someone else has also felt this terrible and survived.

Watch for Signs of Guilt Feelings

One emotion (or perhaps it is a judgment) which children often feel in the midst of tragedy is guilt. Children perceive the world as revolving around them. So, if Mommy and Daddy separate, it must be because "I wasn't a good girl." Or maybe, "If I hadn't run through the house, Mommy wouldn't have become sick and our baby wouldn't have been born too soon."

This is really the only way a child can perceive things. It is very hard for them to understand that bad things just happen without being caused by any person.

Your job is to reassure the child that you understand why he feels that way, while also telling him your perception of the situation—that Mommy and Daddy had a lot of disagreements and couldn't live together, and it had nothing to do with the child. Or that the baby got sick inside Mommy, and that would have happened even if he had played as quietly as a mouse.

Be aware that the child may have received "blaming" messages from important adults. Unfortunately, this happens often. Adults, frustrated and tired, say things like, "Now look what you've done!" and little people take them at their word. So it is often useful, if you perceive serious and strong guilt feelings in your child, to ask her why she thinks she might be to blame. Did she hear something which made her think that? Listen carefully; the child may give you good insight into how you can help.

These books are all designed to reflect the attitude that no child is responsible for tragedy. There is never a hint of that concept, and each book contains a solid explanation of why the tragedy did happen. If you think that guilt is a factor for your child, you might want to ask him if he thinks the child in the story is at fault, and that will help you either to understand his perspective, or to compare his reality with that of the child in the story. Guilt feelings usually don't go away in one meeting, but eventually, with continued support and affirmation, they can be alleviated.

Fidelity, presence, a listening ear, respect, and a willingness to affirm—these are the best ways to help. Now, sit back and read the story. Let it touch you. Look at the questions only after reading the story. When you are with your child, don't use the questions like a school examination. Use them only to begin the conversation. For example, "Why do you suppose Morgan's Mommy wanted a service for Marissa? I wonder if the family felt better after the service?"

Enjoy this time with your special child; remember, friends who can speak about painful things grow closer together. We hope these books will be gifts for your relationship.

Notes about *Morgan's Baby Sister*

This story is designed to draw the reader into the family's joy as the new baby is expected. Sonogram pictures, baby furniture, names—these are all part of a normal pregnancy. The family is real and loving, and everything seems almost too good to be true.

When tragedy strikes, the family is devastated but not unable to cope. Neighbors help, and somehow, they get through the first few days. The reader and listener feel their pain with them.

The most important part of the story begins when Mommy comes home from the hospital. Morgan asks her if she said goodbye to Marissa. The adult suddenly realizes that the child has named a deep need. How the family takes care of the need is also important. They share the time with others who love them. They support and plan together. They draw on their faith background. They do not rush each other but allow much time for grieving. Even after all the excitement of the memorial service, when all the neighbors are back to their normal routines, the pain remains, and the family talks about that.

Morgan's Baby Sister is about an experience common to many families. Krissy's parents have experienced it, and so they understand how Morgan's family feels. Friends help each other.

Krissy grieves for the baby sister she never knew. Her mother cries, even though their baby died a long time ago. Marissa's and Krissy's baby sisters are both acknowledged as part of their families, and Krissy names her sister "Joanna."

All of these experiences are healthy, but they are too often neglected when a baby dies before or shortly after birth. We deny ourselves the time and rituals which can heal. We "get on with life" as if this can do away with the pain. We often completely neglect the grief of siblings, assuming that the baby wasn't "real" to them.

Morgan's Baby Sister addresses issues faced by most families, opens the pathways for conversation, and suggests effective ways of coping with the tragedy of newborn death.

Regarding Balloon Releases

There has been environmental concern over balloon releases (such as the one Morgan's family participates in during the memorial service) because there is a risk of the deflated balloons attracting feeding birds and ocean life. We believe, however, there is no other ritual symbol for "letting go" as therapeutically effective in encouraging the grief process. If you choose to use this symbol with grieving people you love, please be aware of this concern and limit the number of balloons to one for each mourner. Please also be aware that there is a much greater danger with Mylar balloons, which do not deteriorate naturally.

Helium has a time-limited life. Balloons that do not rise are not a good symbol. If you choose to include balloons as part of your ritual, be sure they are inflated just before you begin. Some people like to attach cards bearing an appropriate name or message. If you choose to do this, it might be wise to experiment the day before to ascertain what weight card the balloons will carry.

As an alternative, though perhaps more time-consuming in planning and less "cleansing" in the grieving process, you may consider releasing doves at an appropriate time in the service.

Questions for Discussion

1. What were some of the things Morgan and her Mommy and Daddy did to get ready for Marissa? Why do you suppose they did all that?

2. What happened to Marissa?

3. How did Morgan and her Mommy and Daddy feel when Marissa died? How did they help each other get through this tough time?

4. Why did Morgan's Mommy want a service for Marissa? What were some of the things they did at the service? Do you think it helped them feel a bit better?

5. Why did Morgan invite Krissy to join in the service? Does it ever make you feel better if you have a friend who understands how you are feeling?

6. How were Morgan and her Mommy and Daddy feeling when they had to take down the crib? Why do you think this was hard for them to do? How did they help each other?

7. Has anything in what you have experienced been like the story? What has been helpful to you, or not helpful?